To Mart, with love
K.W.

For my mother
A.K.

Other titles in the *Imagine* series:
Imagine you are a Tiger
Imagine you are a Crocodile
Imagine you are a Dolphin

Text copyright © Karen Wallace 1998
Illustrations copyright © Adrienne Kennaway 1998

The right of Karen Wallace and Adrienne Kennaway to be identified as
the author and illustrator of the Work has been asserted by them in
accordance with the Copyright, Designs and Patents Act 1988.

Published 1998 by Hodder Children's Books
A division of Hodder Headline plc
London NW1 3BH

10 9 8 7 6 5 4 3 2 1

ISBN   0340 678356(PB)
0340 678348(HB)

Printed in Hong Kong

Imagine you are an
ORANG-UTAN

Karen Wallace

Adrienne Kennaway

Hodder
Children's
Books

A division of Hodder Headline plc

Imagine you are an orang-utan.

A young orang-utan sits in the rain,
In rainforest rain that falls like a torrent.
Her wiry red fur glitters with water.
She breaks off a leaf to use as an umbrella.

Imagine you are an orang-utan.

The rainstorm is over.

She swings on the branch,

drops her leaf to the ground.

A young orang-utan crouches and watches her mother.
Her mother is feeding the newly born baby.
He nuzzles and sucks and clings to her belly.

Imagine you are an orang-utan, living in the forest.

In a green steamy forest which smells of wet earth.

Curtains of cobwebs droop between creepers.

Leaves hang like wet washing then dry in the sun.

High in a treetop, a hornbill is feeding.
Mangoes and figs bounce on the ground.
A young orang-utan learns to
follow the hornbill,
To listen for the whistle of its
fast-beating wings.

Where a hornbill finds fruit, there is more to be eaten.
A young orang-utan climbs after her mother,
Follows her path as she leaps through the branches.

A red-haired orang-utan stuffs
her mouth full of mangoes.
She smears the sweet fruit all over her face.
Her belly is bulging.
She leans back and scratches.
Her mother and brother rest in the sun.

Imagine you are an orang-utan.

When the sun sinks in the forest,

She practises building her nest for the night.

She picks a forked branch the way her mother has taught her,

Grabs twigs and small branches (and perhaps one more mango)

Weaves the branches together with handfuls of leaves.

Above her, her mother has built her nest faster.
She sleeps with her baby warm at her side.

Imagine you are an orang-utan.

She's safe, high in her leaf-bed.

Night comes.

The forest echoes with noises.

Far below a tiger slinks through the creepers,

Claws the bark of a tree and growls loudly with hunger.

Imagine you are an orang-utan.

Sun spreads through the forest.

A slow-swinging orang-utan plays in the branches.

Her feet grip like hands.

Her arms are strong as legs.

She's sure as a dancer in her world in the treetops.

A young orang-utan is chewing a leaf-bud.

Her mother is teaching her brother to climb.

She spits out the leaf-bud,

And pulls a face in the sunshine.

Far off in the forest, an orang-utan is calling.

She swings through the trees to start a life on her own.

Imagine you are an orang-utan.